mini saga
competition
for Primary Schools from Young Writers

Tiny Tales

Warwickshire &
The West Midlands

First published in Great Britain in 2007 by
Young Writers, Remus House, Coltsfoot Drive,
Peterborough, PE2 9JX
Tel (01733) 890066 Fax (01733) 313524
All Rights Reserved

© Copyright Contributors 2007
SB ISBN 978-1-84431-369-3

Foreword

Young Writers was established in 1991, with the aim of encouraging the children and young adults of today to think and write creatively. Our latest primary school competition, *Tiny Tales*, posed an exciting challenge for these young authors: to write, in no more than fifty words, a story encompassing a beginning, a middle and an end. We call this the mini saga.

Tiny Tales Warwickshire & The West Midlands is our latest offering from the wealth of young talent that has mastered this incredibly challenging form. With such an abundance of imagination, humour and ability evident in such a wide variety of stories, these young writers cannot fail to enthral and excite with every tale.

Contents

Meriden CE Primary School, Coventry

Norfolk House School, Birmingham

Priors Field Primary School, Kenilworth

Robin Hood Primary School, Birmingham

The Mini Sagas

Going Up!

What was that? Something horrifying was standing in front of me. It was tall, but on the inside it was like a prison. If it didn't open there was no escape.
Taking a deep breath I stepped inside. It closed its gaping mouth, swallowing me!
The lift surged up … up …

Kelsey Johnson (11)
Alderman's Green Community School, Coventry

13

Harry Potter

Harry Potter was a baby when his parents were killed by the dark Lord Voldemort. At eleven he got a letter from Hogwarts. The next month he went to Hogwarts; Harry made two friends, Ron and Hermione. Dumbledore was headmaster of Hogwart's. He was kind and polite to everyone.

Zahra Bibi (11)
Birchfield Community School, Birmingham

14

Petey

Petey, or PT3000 as he is known to the factory,
is there to help with all the household chores.
Meanwhile Mum and Dad are busy with the
Ultra Reality machine.
Only Sophie and Sam can see that Petey is
behaving in a very peculiar way for a machine
…

Sufiyan Sheikh (8)
Birchfield Community School, Birmingham

Miley's Great Sleepover

Miley was going to have a sleepover. She invited all her friends. When they came they all quickly rushed upstairs.
All of the girls had lots of food and drink. When it was time to go to sleep everyone was tired but they still all had a pillow fight.

Fatima Delair (9)
Birchfield Community School, Birmingham

Santa Claus Forever

Everything is going wrong for Santa Claus on Christmas Eve because a brick has dropped on his head, one of his reindeer is sick and his trousers have caught fire.
Maybe it's time to retire, but what will the new Santa Claus be like, the man from Mega-Fun Corporation?

Junaid Hussain (7)
Birchfield Community School, Birmingham

James And
The Giant Peach

Until he was four James Henry Trotter had a
happy life. He lived peacefully with his mother
and father in a beautiful house beside the sea.
There were always plenty of other children for
him to play with and there was a sandy beach
where he could play.

Faheem Ahmed (8)
Birchfield Community School, Birmingham

18

The Dark Woods
Of The Witch

Little Sophie was playing in her back garden.
Rain thundered down. When it was bright
again, Sophie went to the woods to explore.
Sophie did not know a witch was watching her.
'Ha, a girl I can use for my spell.'
She kidnapped Sophie and turned her into a
frog.

Rukaya Hadi (8)
Birchfield Community School, Birmingham

Little Jackie
And Her Dad

Little Jackie was hiding behind a tree. She heard a noise, it came closer until it was behind Jackie. She screamed.

Her mother asked, 'What is the matter?' She pointed but there was nothing there.

Her mother went closer and her dad jumped out. 'I scared you!'

'Oh no, yes!'

Habibah Mahmood (8)
Birchfield Community School, Birmingham

20

Beautiful Mermaids

Rani swam down through the turquoise water until her belly touched the sandy bottom of the seabed. Then she did a quick flip with her tail so that she somersaulted backwards again. 'Show off!' she heard as she flicked her hair out of her eyes.

She turned around, 'Mum!'

Aaliyah Unia (8)
Birchfield Community School, Birmingham

21

Sharp

So where was he? He said he'd get it and be here at nine sharp. No one was there. Something howled somewhere. Cold shivers went up my spine.
Unexpectedly the sound of rustling leaves entered my ears. I hesitated and looked back. Suddenly a sharp object sank into my back!

Ismail Mohammed (11)
Birchfield Community School, Birmingham

22

The Dragon Tree

Kipper has got a book, he asks Chip to read it. Chip reads it, the key glows, they are in a forest!
A dragon chases them. The key glows again and they're back home again.
Kipper has a little bone in his hand. Kipper shows Chip and they both smile.

Khalil Saiyed (11)
Birchfield Community School, Birmingham

23

The Count Of Monte Cristo

Count of Monte Cristo tries to take five million pounds off Bardon Dangulars but Bardon Dangulars doesn't give it to him. He tries to kill the Count of Monte Cristo. Abbie helps Monte Cristo and they kill Bardon Dangulars and take five million pounds and run to the police station.

Awzair Chaudhrey (11)
Birchfield Community School, Birmingham

24

The Haunted Attic

Gemma landed in an attic with her friend Lucy, it was so dark in there. The door kept on opening and closing. They both screamed but no one would hear because no one was in the house.

So they were stuck in the attic for the rest of their lives!

Tafima Akhtar (10)
Birchfield Community School, Birmingham

April Fool's Day

There I was! Emily told me to be here. I heard something then someone ran past. *Argh!* There was something stamping. 'Emily, is that you?' I said but nobody answered. I ran out, there she was. 'Were you April Fool?'
'Yes!'
But then who was inside?

Tanzila Masoud (10)
Birchfield Community School, Birmingham

The Football Match

Jim had three tickets for the big match so he
went to Old Trafford. His team, Man United,
won while he was eating popcorn. 'Hooray for
Man United,' he yelled.
On the way home he dreamt that he was Man
United's captain.
What a match, he thought!

Safwaan Afsar (10)
Birchfield Community School, Birmingham

27

The Princess And The Pea

There was a princess who went away. It so happened that she had to sleep at a palace. The bed was made up with many mattresses with a pea at the bottom. When the princess awoke next morning, she saw the pea, then married the prince and lived happily.

Siddiqah Teladia (10)
Birchfield Community School, Birmingham

28

Goldilocks And The Three Bears

Goldilocks saw a house, there was porridge, there were three bowls. Baby Bear's was just right. She went to the next room, there were three chairs, Baby Bear's was just … *oops!* She broke it. She went upstairs, there were three beds. Baby Bear's was just right.
The bears returned, *'Argh!'*

Sarah Shazad (10)
Birchfield Community School, Birmingham

The Horror

Tom shivered with fear. He closed his eyes
wishing the terrifying faces would disappear. He
covered his ears, ignoring the screaming.
He'd gone in, where's the way out? He felt a
chill down his back. Was he dead? The doors
flew open.
He never went on the ghost train again!

Uzair Hussain (10)
Bordesley Village Primary School, Birmingham

The Girl
And The Figure

She opened the creaky door. She saw a black slim figure lurking around. She felt a cool but slow breeze brushing through her hair. She turned around to go home but the door disappeared! There were now only four walls and that spooky figure lurking around! You scared yet?

Hifsah Ahmed (9)
Bordesley Village Primary School, Birmingham

31

The Terrifying Touch

One night I went to sleep, I felt something touch my back. I ignored it. It touched me again, I was petrified. I dozed, I heard moaning, everything went black.
I looked out my window and heard miaowing, a cat, black like a demon's eyes.
I turned around … *Huh … !*

Olivia Ruth Spencer-James (10)
Bordesley Village Primary School, Birmingham

The Lightning Widow's Ghost

Bill's mom screamed while the violent lightning flashed like a blowing bulb. They looked out the window and noticed a strange figure walking towards the house. *Knock, knock.*
They opened the door, standing there was an old widow. She'd dropped dead and her ghost still remains haunting the house.

Khagen Douglas (10)
Bordesley Village Primary School, Birmingham

33

A Strange Dream

One gloomy night a light came from the sky,
it was green. I stepped towards the light. I
was going back to my house when the light
attracted me into a UFO.
Suddenly an alien was about to operate on me
until an astronaut saved me.
Then I woke up!

Abubaker Hussain (10)
Bordesley Village Primary School, Birmingham

The Haunted House

As the sun was just setting, Luke decided to go for a walk. Luke was a learned boy. He had thick wavy locks and eyes as blue as the sea. After a while Luke was outside a creaky old door. He pushed the door with fear and ended up pale!

Amaal Ellahi (10)
Bordesley Village Primary School, Birmingham

The Ghost Train

'Argh!' Ghosts were popping up from nowhere. Blood was dripping from the ceilings. I was terrified! There was no escape. I tried calling for help but nothing! I tried to get out but I was stuck.
Then daylight. The ghost train stopped. I hugged and hugged my mother with pleasure!

Labonnie Haider
Bordesley Village Primary School, Birmingham

The Ghost Train

The ghost train sped off to the top, then suddenly went down. I saw blood dripping from the ceiling. The ghost popped out from nowhere. Rats were scurrying beside me. Bogeymen started shouting. The skeletons screamed and one sat in the seat next to me! The trip finished …

Akram Ali (8)
Bordesley Village Primary School, Birmingham

Making A Snowman

I made two balls, one big, one small. I stuck them together and got some buttons and made a mouth and eyes. Then I got two sticks and made two arms. Then I gave him a hat and said, 'Goodbye!'

Mohamed Shaiban (10)
Bordesley Village Primary School, Birmingham

The Ghost In The Dark

You might be braver than me. There is this
ghost that is frightening me.
One dark night it crept up to me and leapt on
my legs ... I screamed, *'Argh!'*
Then I noticed it had fur. I suddenly realised,
'Phew! it is only the cat!'

Noha Said (9)
Bordesley Village Primary School, Birmingham

A Surprise Of Your Life

One dark, dark day in a dark, dark road, I lost my mom. Then I saw a strange-looking home! I went towards it. The door opened and I never even touched it. Then I looked behind the door. It was my mum and before I saw her … 'Boo!'

Paige Ridgway (9)
Bordesley Village Primary School, Birmingham

Scary Story

One dark, spooky night a shy little girl called Kim looked out of her window. She tiptoed downstairs and ran across the wet, dark street. She opened the door, then a rattlesnake appeared and said, 'You have to get out of here or *he* will appear!'

Abigail Campbell (10)
Bordesley Village Primary School, Birmingham

41

YoungWriters

Lauren And
The Babysitter

Lauren's parents went out and left Lauren with
the babysitter. She never cared about Lauren.
Lauren went upstairs to her bedroom and heard
a knock on the window. She checked to see
who it was but there was no one there.
A final knock … followed by a scream!

Javeria Ali (10)
Bordesley Village Primary School, Birmingham

42

The Disappearing Of The House

Lightning shot in different directions and the thick white layers attacked innocent children. Homes being brought down.
But there was a rather unusual-looking figure heading towards another house. White mist, bloodshot eyes, scaring off anything that dropped in its path.
Two knocks on the door, the house vanished!

Ali Khaliq (10)
Bordesley Village Primary School, Birmingham

The Bloodthirsty Tiger

A girl called Kate went into a jungle looking for animals but suddenly Kate became scared.
Roar! roared a bloodthirsty tiger.
'Argh!' yelled Kate.
She kept walking until she saw a tiger coming closer to eat.
Gobble! The tiger gobbled Kate!

Krish Gohil (9)
Bordesley Village Primary School, Birmingham

The Witch In The Girl

One night the girl went to the park, she was terrified. She walked by a bottle, she kicked it up the tree.

As she walked, she heard a noise, as she walked even more, she saw a witch. That witch came at her in a flash … she was a horrible monster!

Mustafa Ali (10)
Bordesley Village Primary School, Birmingham

Zombie Nightmare

I woke up, heart racing, sweating like it was pouring rain. The devilish things I remembered, zombies ganging around me. I looked at my legs, the weird thing was that my legs weren't there!

'Argh!' I was grabbed by the arms. I turned pale

...

I was turning into a zombie!

Ashley Jones (10)
Bordesley Village Primary School, Birmingham

46

The Bloody Vampire

Once lived two boys called Solomon and John.
Next door lived the Bloody Vampire.
John asked, 'Why do they call him The Bloody
Vampire?'
'Because he sucks people's brain blood.'
'That's nasty,' replied John.
He woke up early next morning, he thought, *I'm
going back to that vampire house.*

Jamil Ahmed (10)
Bordesley Village Primary School, Birmingham

The Lost Woods

'Come out, come out, wherever you are.'
The girl ran as fast as she could. All her hair
stood up on end. The bloodshot eyes and the
blood dripping from his mouth frightened her.
'I've got you now!'
From that day on the little girl was never found
again.

Sajeda Parvin (9)
Bordesley Village Primary School, Birmingham

48

Ghost Freaks

'You can run but you can't hide,' screamed a horrendous voice.
He sounded like an animal. I was petrified.
Suddenly everything went black. I woke up but everything was different.
There were two holes in my neck and I was pale. The monster that had done this was thin air …

Saim Haider (9)
Bordesley Village Primary School, Birmingham

The Lady

You can't run from me you ugly girl, I'm going
to get you with my hands. Zoe, you killed me,
I'm going to kill you with my bloodthirsty mouth.
You'd better count to five. *Boo!* You are dead …
That was delicious, I want some more now!

Aleena Neelufar (10)
Bordesley Village Primary School, Birmingham

My Dead Brother

My home is the only place I can feel safe with
these murderers around, including me …
I murdered my brother with my shotgun but my
neighbour got the blame!
'Jack, Jack, wake up,' said Jackie, Jack's mum.

James Devaney (10)
Claverdon Primary School, Claverdon

51

A Stroll Through The Woods

I strolled into the gloomy wood and I heard a rustle. I jumped backwards.
A man in a black jumper came out. He put a gun to my head. As I shouted, I ran but there was a river.
I fell …

Adam Williams (10)
Claverdon Primary School, Claverdon

The Death Of Asmir

'Dad, why do we have to go?' Asmir cried.
'They are going to clean us out,' Dad gulped.
We are already clean though,' Asmir said, he
was confused.
'Go to sleep, you are going to be evacuated
tomorrow. Go to sleep,' Dad sobbed.
'OK,' Asmir said quietly.
Bang!

Charlie Hargreaves (10)
Claverdon Primary School, Claverdon

53

The Greatest Wizard

Once, there lived a puppy, Ben. His owner, the greatest wizard, cast a spell on the puppy so when he grew up he would be able to talk to any animal in the world.
Years passed and finally he could talk to animals,
but Ben could only speak to fish!

Aimée Maritz (10)
Claverdon Primary School, Claverdon

Murder In The Dark

I sat in my bed because my mum and dad had gone out for the night. I heard a funny noise, a creaking of my door!
As my room was massive, I hid in my cupboard. He opened the cupboard door. A dagger came towards my body.
I froze … !

Alyx Reed (10)
Claverdon Primary School, Claverdon

55

The Deserted Street

I walked down the deserted street, nothing in sight. I stumbled and tripped, fell over, and there beside me was a man lying face down, dead!
I got up and saw a blood-covered battlefield. It was horrible! I carried on walking. Suddenly, something grabbed me …
I screamed *silently!*

Jessica Wade (10)
Claverdon Primary School, Claverdon

Hodenski

A hundred years ago there was a wizard called Hodenski. His spells were always going wrong. One day he saw a purple cat stuck in a tree so he cast a weird and wonderful spell that accidentally blew the cat up like a balloon ...

Ella Wilkinson (10)
Claverdon Primary School, Claverdon

An Amazing Trip
To Colourful Jungle

Once I decided to go to Colourful Jungle. An
early morning, oh no!
I finally arrived, pulled back luscious leaves
and saw a jungle with colours everywhere.
Suddenly a monkey, multicoloured, jumped
out. He gave me a horrific shock! We became
best friends.
Argh! A bright green monster's jumped out!

Rebecca Knott (10)
Claverdon Primary School, Claverdon

Missing Nemo

'Dad, time for school!' Nemo shouted.
'OK then,' Dad replied tiredly.
Marlin and Nemo, the clownfish, swam to the
school drop-off point. Then Nemo saw a rusty
boat, he swam towards it. He touched it and
suddenly, he vanished!
Nemo was never seen ever again!

Amy Read (10)
Claverdon Primary School, Claverdon

The Alien Egg

There, glistening beneath a spiky bramble
bush, was a bright blue egg. What was it?
Suddenly, it shook! It was hatching! I panicked.
What was it? What would I do with it?
Then it started to crack, I wanted to bolt!
A slimy, bony claw appeared from the inside
… *'Argh!'*

Edward Hardy (10)
Claverdon Primary School, Claverdon

Haunted Reality

Dear Diary, today was horrific. I can't live in a place so damp and dark. My family's unsafe. Everywhere I look someone's dead or dying! Every night I hear blood-curdling screams that shiver down my spine. Every time I open a window I smell rotting flesh.
We must leave!

Ria Matthews (9)
Claverdon Primary School, Claverdon

Barking Mad

One day three dogs travelled with their owners
to a barking competition in Warwick. The dogs'
names were Ben, Lottie and Megan.
Finally they arrived. There were three dogs
competing. The show started and they all
barked their heads off.
The prize was a doggie bone! *Woof!*

Ellie Wells (10)
Claverdon Primary School, Claverdon

Love Hurts

He's gone, he's really, really gone! He told me
he'd go but I never really thought he would. I
love him and I miss him. I want him back. I've
got to get him back!
I'll fight for him, I will. If only he heard me say, 'I
love you.'

Verity Bacon (10)
Claverdon Primary School, Claverdon

63

The Wrong Spell

'Argh! My hands are green,' the wizard shouted.
'What is it?' All of a sudden I saw my hands
making the spell! I loaded the spell with lots of
stuff, even a chicken, it went mad!
I drank it so quickly, then my hands … How?

Katie Brown (10)
Claverdon Primary School, Claverdon

Three Little Pigs

One day three little pigs went home; their mother said, 'Go, make your own houses!' They made them but suddenly a wolf came. So all of the pigs ended up in one house where the wolf came down the chimney and landed in a pot of boiling water!

Elizabeth Sear (10)
Claverdon Primary School, Claverdon

65

Three Piglets

Mother Pig told her young, 'Build a house of
your own, there's no room here!'
Wolfie came, so the first pig ran to the second
pig's house. Then they both ran to the third
pig's house.
Wolfie jumped down the brick chimney and
died!

Alisha Teasdale (10)
Claverdon Primary School, Claverdon

War And Peace

Screaming as I fall five thousand feet from an aircraft, loud gunfire noises fill the air. Below me the ocean lies like a black hole of death! Tears streak down my face as I think of my family. As I hit the water I am powerless. It is the end!

Emma Kensett (10)
Claverdon Primary School, Claverdon

67

This Is Not War, It's Murder!

I clung to my rifle, I was caked in mud and filth.
I was breathing heavily. Suddenly I heard a
whistle, a whistle of despair!
I climbed over the top of the trench, fired,
then ran as fast as I could, but I fell over and
knocked myself out, cold …

William Thorneywork (10)
Claverdon Primary School, Claverdon

Camping Nightmare

Frankie couldn't believe it! His father lying in a pool of blood! It was as though everything had frozen, apart from something that looked like a furry, brown, strange tree stump.
Suddenly, Frankie realised, he darted back to the car … but it was too late!

Jasmine Ambrose-Brown (10)
Claverdon Primary School, Claverdon

Deathly Disaster

It was quiet, too quiet. I gazed around me, everyone was screaming. Then I realised I was too!
The plane swerved and zoomed towards the roaring waves. My face went white and a warm tear rolled down my cold cheek.
This was the end, *'Argh!'*

Lottie Panting (10)
Claverdon Primary School, Claverdon

The Killer Spider

I saw it first out of the corner of my eye. It was a small dot to start with, it grew bigger and bigger as it moved towards me. I shook with fear as it almost touched me!
Then it stopped … under the glass that Dad trapped it with.

Mia Eaden (9)
Dickens Heath Primary School, Solihull

71

Yuk!

I entered the hall. I sat down for a long, long time. I got closer and closer and closer and closer and closer and closer, until I saw it! It was horrible … I hate school dinners!

Olivia Brown (8)
Dickens Heath Primary School, Solihull

The Monster And Tom

Once there was a monster that killed everyone.
And there once was a boy who saved everyone.
One day they met and the monster tried to
kill everyone, so the boy grabbed his sword
and shield and stabbed the monster. Blood
splattered everywhere.
A huge cheer went around everyone!

Beth Woodward (10)
Four Oaks Primary School, Sutton Coldfield

73

Revenge Of The Living Dead

One day Ben and John went canoeing and fell asleep. When they woke up they were approaching an island. They couldn't see through the mist but it was Skull Island! Whoever went in, never came out! They explored around. They were captured. Luckily they escaped from a fire!

Shivras Sisodia (10)
Four Oaks Primary School, Sutton Coldfield

74

The Dragon Slayer Is No More

In a mythical land, King Arthur ruled with his knights. All was well until a slayer came to Camelot. He killed all the dragons except one. They had a bloody battle. A dragon rider killed the slayer and that was the end of the dragon slayer!

Jack Wolverson (10)
Four Oaks Primary School, Sutton Coldfield

Bishua The Demon

George and Rupert were bullied at school by Bonjo. They were shipped away to a school for bullied children.
When they grew up they became detectives. They were given a mission at Matteo's castle to destroy the evil demon Bishua.
Rupert and George got a chainsaw and sawed him up!

Tom Williams (10)
Four Oaks Primary School, Sutton Coldfield

Monster In My Bedroom

There was a monster in my bedroom hiding under my bed. That monster scared me. One night I had a nightmare about him. I woke up, I heard noises. It was him!
'Joey, Joey.' He was calling me by my name! He suddenly jumped at me …

Conor Raymond Benbow
Four Oaks Primary School, Sutton Coldfield

77

It's Just The Beginning

Once there was a girl, Molly, she was a superhero at night, but during the day she was a jerk.

There were three baddies (elves). They planned to steal money from the bank. They did and Molly saw them. She kicked them and phoned the police.

Now they're in jail!

Claudia Mewis (10)
Four Oaks Primary School, Sutton Coldfield

Monster Under My Bed

Once upon a time there was a boy called
Conor, he had browny-black hair and brown
eyes. He liked playing on his PSP.
One day Conor woke up, started playing on his
PSP, then suddenly Conor heard a voice saying,
'Look under your bed!'
Conor looked under the bed ...

Oliver Copson (9)
Four Oaks Primary School, Sutton Coldfield

Monster From The Deep

Tom and George were extremely bad people.
They built a monster. It was remote controlled.
One day it sucked up a whole river!
Then from the sky came Sir Rupert. He slew the
monster with his sword and it lay dead on the
ground.
'Hooray,' shouted the people, 'we're saved!'

Rupert Daniels (10)
Four Oaks Primary School, Sutton Coldfield

Magic Mayhem

Chrissy and Lucy were playing outside. When Allegra asked if she could play, Lucy said, 'No!' Allegra started to use her magic on them. Later on, all of them had used their magic. Suddenly the fairy queen came in and told them off! They never quarrelled again after that!

Marni Chhokar (9)
Four Oaks Primary School, Sutton Coldfield

Untitled

Once upon a time, lived a man who owned a sweet shop. All the children in the village loved going to the sweet shop. A girl called Emily bought a pear drop because she was having a bad dream.
One day the pear drop worked … Emily was happy again!

Joanne Kitteridge (9)
Four Oaks Primary School, Sutton Coldfield

82

The Three Little Piglets

The houses were being built by the three little piglets. The wolf shouted to them in the distance, 'Hi piglets!'
'Quick,' whispered the first piglet. 'Get Mr Wolf away.' And they went into their houses.
A big gust of wind blew two houses away as Mr Wolf sadly walked away.

Matthew McElroy (10)
Four Oaks Primary School, Sutton Coldfield

83

Sam Kills The Dragon

There was a boy called Sam who lived in the forest. One day Sam went to play with his new sword.
Sam heard noises, suddenly a massive monster jumped out, he went to hit Sam but Sam stabbed him with his sword.
Sam went home and went straight to bed.

Rachel Clarke (10)
Four Oaks Primary School, Sutton Coldfield

Untitled

Cinders went into a deep dark forest in a deep dark wood. It was so spooky she fainted and a prince who was walking in the forest saw Cinders on the ground. He kissed her and she said, 'Where am I?'
'You're in the forest with me,' said the prince.

Breana KhunKhun (7)
Graiseley Primary School, Wolverhampton

85

The Shark And The Alligator

The great shark was looking for the mighty alligator. 'I am the beast of the sea!' he growled. 'No one can beat me up,' shouted Shark. At 2 o'clock, Alligator plonked the shark with a rounders bat and took the staff! *'I am king,* ha, ha, ha!' shouted Alligator!

Vijay Patel (8)
Graiseley Primary School, Wolverhampton

Sweet Dreams

I can't believe I'm in Disneyland, where is
everybody?
I'm alone, I'm going on every roller coaster. I
stay there for ages! *Wow,* look at that horse
ride, I want a go on it now. 'Giddy up boy!'
'Drake, Drake, Drake, wake up. Drake!'
'Uh, Mum, you spoilt my dream!'

Simone McKen (8)
Graiseley Primary School, Wolverhampton

Untitled

The penguins woke up and went downstairs to
have some cereal. They heard noises, *creak!*
Bang!
'Go and see what that was!'
'Oh no! We'll go together.'
'*Argh!* Ghosts!'
It was Mum and Dad … 'You scared us!'
'Hey, it's Hallowe'en night!'
'Where's our costumes?'

Capreece Miranda (8)
Graiseley Primary School, Wolverhampton

Grannyhood

Once there was a granny who wanted to be different so she decided to act young.
The next day Granny thought she would have a skate. She nicked her granddaughter's skates and went rolling down the street! Granny was good!
Then she wanted to be Granny again, so she changed.

Amy Hollywood (7)
Graiseley Primary School, Wolverhampton

An Accident In Walsall Bus Station

On Monday at noon, something terrible happened. An Arriva bus crashed into a TWM bus! The Arriva driver told us he didn't mean to crash. The bus went out of his control. Seven people were injured including pedestrians who were crossing. Even the Arriva driver was badly hurt!

Chantelle White (10)
Hatherton Primary School, Walsall

The Magic Spell That Went Wrong

There was a sly wizard who cast a spell and it went wrong, as usual. I found him in his wizard hut. One day he showed me a spell and it went wrong again. I helped him fix it and it worked and never went wrong again in his life.

Abbey Caulton (10)
Hatherton Primary School, Walsall

Untitled

Once upon a time a lady always thought she could do magic then one day when she was alone in her house she went into the garden, got her things and tried to do some magic. She got it wrong, she tried again and got it right. She was overjoyed!

Shanie Whitticase (10)
Hatherton Primary School, Walsall

Loch Ness Monster

Click! went the camera. *Yes! I've finally got a picture of the Loch Ness monster* thought Alison as she went to Asda to have the photos developed. The picture was great; when she got the photo she handed it to the 'News' This made her very, very famous!

Chloe Ferguson (10)
Hatherton Primary School, Walsall

93

Untitled

'Hey, my name's Pirate Cooper and I'm small with long hair, brown eyes and a patch on my eye. Can I ask you something? Why don't pirates smoke?'

'I don't know, why pirates don't smoke?'

'Because they've got a patch, *Ha! Ha! Ha! Ha! Ha!*'

Billie Jo Cooper (10)
Hatherton Primary School, Walsall

94

Monster Business

One day when I came home I heard a funny noise. I went up to my bedroom to solve the mystery. Standing there was a monster with huge claws and a hairy face. *'Argh!'* I yelled. *'Rrrrooaar!'* boomed the monster.
My little brother was the horrible monster causing mayhem!

James Ellis (10)
Hatherton Primary School, Walsall

95

The Creepy House

It was a dark and stormy night. The house was dark and creepy. As I was creeping through the yard, I heard a spooky noise. I creaked open the door. I felt terrified because I saw a skeleton was there.
I was *doomed!*

Reuben Egan (9)
Knightlow CE Primary School, Rugby

The Ghost Story

One mysterious night there was heavy rain, with thunder and lightning. A guy found a haunted house in the middle of nowhere. He went upstairs to investigate. At the top of the stairs there was a ghost weeping with a soundless scream but a big *giant* roar!

Callum Gardner (9)
Knightlow CE Primary School, Rugby

The Magic Pine Cone

One day, Paige found a pine cone, but it wasn't brown, it was yellow. Mum said it was just an ordinary pine cone but in a way Paige thought it was special. She touched it but nothing happened!
Suddenly a tiny beautiful fairy appeared …
'Who are you?' asked Paige anxiously.

Brittany Wood (8)
Knightlow CE Primary School, Rugby

98

Murder In The Dark

I was walking through the graveyard when suddenly, at the back of the church, I saw the Grim Reaper! He stood over me and breathed in my face. I tried to run but with his magic, he locked the door!
I was *doomed!*

Ben Oliver (9)
Knightlow CE Primary School, Rugby

Hydrophobia

We are back at North High, my high school. I've
been invited to a swimming party. I don't know
what to do because I can't swim! My best friend
has hydrophobia. He has an excuse.
Hopefully Ben the bully won't be there.
The school knows him as 'the crusher'. *Yug!*

**Lydia Aaron, Lydia Smith
& Courtney Robinson (9)**
Knightlow CE Primary School, Rugby

The Sneezing Rescue

The prince walked up to the long dragon that was asleep. The dragon was snoring loudly so the prince stepped bravely into the mouth of the dragon and walked down to where the princess lay. He tickled the dragon's throat and, with a mighty sneeze, the dragon sneezed them out!

Harriet Jack (10)
Knightlow CE Primary School, Rugby

Jamangi

Bang! went the gun. He was here for the game.
I ran as fast as I could down the street, through
the door and hid.
The door swung open, he stood looking at me.
He stepped out of the shadows. First a boot,
then another boot, *'Help!'* I ...
'Hi Dad!'

Lana Bass (11)
Meriden CE Primary School, Coventry

102

The Get-Back

A rock came through the window of my new BMW X5. Dave was trying to get me back for when I drove into his car. I swerved round onto the beach, just missing little children! I was so frightened, I jumped …

Then I realised I was dreaming. I was glad!

Benjamin Andrews (11)
Meriden CE Primary School, Coventry

The Monster

Crash! Bang! Boom! I heard feet creeping through the hall. I saw a big shadow moving slowly. I was hugging my sister in fear. I wondered what was going on.

Bash! went a window. *'Argh!* it's a monster, run, hide!'

'Look, it's Dad dressing up!'

'You really scared me Dad!'

Emily Betts (11)
Meriden CE Primary School, Coventry

Crash Down

Vrooom! Monster trucks, lorries and vans zoomed past. Kassy didn't understand, she'd only had the car repaired yesterday! She stepped back as the traffic sped up and mad swerving vehicles came towards her, she sighed as splodges of wet, cold water poured on her face. Finally the AA …

Grace Spalding (11)
Meriden CE Primary School, Coventry

105

Moving Steps

I took a daring step closer, sweat dripping from me. I froze. Should I? I heard laughing. *'Argh!'* I slipped …
No longer in control, I was going down. I trembled! It seemed never-ending. Then I ran down, not thinking I'd stopped.
It was finished, my nightmare of escalators, over!

Charlotte Nicklin (11)
Meriden CE Primary School, Coventry

The Drop

I had to do it, I couldn't be a wimp!
As I climbed the steps, I felt one million metres
high! I went a step backwards but Billie pushed
me up. I looked over to see the drop. This was
it, I was going to do it …
I hate slides!

Georgia Peglar (11)
Meriden CE Primary School, Coventry

It's A Miracle

Hearts thumping, the two parents sat frozen
in hospital. Sweat trickled slowly down their
necks. They listened as a doctor walked down
the corridor. Their son was really ill! He'd got a
disease that could kill him!
'I'm pleased to say that you son is very well, Mr
Hitler!'

Timothy Smith (11)
Meriden CE Primary School, Coventry

The Death Of The Wolf

One dark night in the forest were Red Riding Hoodie and his crew. The wolf was walking through. *Bang!* The crew jumped on him. When he got up he was so dizzy he fell to the ground. He was shot by the posse. Poor scary wolf!

Macaulay Phillips (11)
Meriden CE Primary School, Coventry

Joanne's Birthday

Ring, ring, Joanne's alarm clock went, it was her birthday today. She'd opened one present yesterday because she was anxious about her tenth birthday.

Joanne didn't enjoy her horrid little brother getting presents on *her* birthday. 'I mean, why is he so important?' She will get him back some way!

Adrienne Lindeque (11)
Meriden CE Primary School, Coventry

Out In The Dark

Crash! The tennis ball hit the lighthouse, everywhere went black. Sam looked around, nobody was about. Sam tiptoed into the multicoloured house, it was pitch-black inside. How on earth was she going to switch it back on before her dad came back on the boat …? He was behind her!

Rebecca Court (10)
Meriden CE Primary School, Coventry

The Banging

George was in the garden when he heard banging from upstairs. He went upstairs but couldn't see anything, but felt a chill run down his spine! He checked every room in the house, even down the stairs. Then he came to his bedroom and in his cupboard, there was … nothing!

Luke Beasley (11)
Meriden CE Primary School, Coventry

Spirit

Spirit ran to see what strange light was there. When Spirit saw the three strange creatures he suddenly realised two of them had woken. Spirit panicked and started to run.
'Hey, why can't I be Spirit and you be the men?'
'Because you do it all wrong.'
'That's not fair!'

Alicia Tredell (10)
Meriden CE Primary School, Coventry

113

The Three Little Pigs And The Big Dead Wolf

The three little pigs were happily relaxing in their garden when the big bad wolf came over the little pigs' fence. The big bad wolf grabbed his axe. He lifted his axe and then *wham!* The wolf was dead on the floor!

Oliver Gambino (10)
Meriden CE Primary School, Coventry

114

Untitled

Mr Bean had to go to the dentist and he was scared, but he still went. He had to have an injection in his mouth, that was why he was frightened.
When he got there he had to wait a long time; eventually he had his injection and was happy!

Ryan Derbyshire (9)
Meriden CE Primary School, Coventry

The Spirits Return

There was once a girl called Holly, she lived in the city. There had been a car crash by the side of a river so one day she went to see who it was.

Someone seemed to be following her so she turned around and *'Argh!'* was all she said.

Chloe Barrett (10)
Meriden CE Primary School, Coventry

Singing Star

Lucy heard the gentle wind from her window hitting the cymbals. The band kept still, everyone was watching. Lucy sang, the band played. They tried their best. Lucy finished the song.
'Well done, you sang with excitement and the band played confidently.'
'The winner is ... Lucy and her band.'

Heidi Garbett (10)
Meriden CE Primary School, Coventry

Deep Dark Bond

Mr Bond was hiding in the shadows. He felt a shiver and heard steps. Bond jumped around and saw Hans Moleman.
James pulled his trigger … nothing!
Moleman did the same.
James threw his gun. There was a *pow!*
Moleman was dead!

Callum Duckers (10)
Meriden CE Primary School, Coventry

118

The Underground

He was trapped, there was no chance he
could get out. Packed into a wooden case and
dropped into a hole thirty metres below the
ground, which was then filled with tarmac later
in the night.
He was slowly suffocating.
He had a limited supply of oxygen, rapidly
running out!

Philip Mulcahy (10)
Meriden CE Primary School, Coventry

119

White Snow And The Six Dwarves (And The Big Hairy Monster)

White Snow was serving carrot soup in little bowls to her six little dwarves.
All of a sudden, *bang! Thud! Crash!* 'Fee fi, fo, fum, I smell the blood of an Englishman!'
'Argh!'
'Billie, give me back that garden gnome, you've stolen one already!' cried Lilly, running after him!

Natalie Flavelle (10)
Meriden CE Primary School, Coventry

The Bang

Jack Sparrow once again had set to sea. He was drinking bottles of rum. His crew was asleep but he wasn't.

Suddenly he heard the *bang* of a cannon. The whole crew jumped out of bed and ran on deck. But all they could see was fog …

Bradley Pinkham (10)
Meriden CE Primary School, Coventry

121

The Girl Who Was Kidnapped

There once lived a family with a little girl.
Suddenly pirates came and took their child;
they took her to an island.
Amazingly she liked the island! Her parents
came to save her but she didn't want to leave
so they built a hut and stayed forever!

Ashleigh Edwards (10)
Meriden CE Primary School, Coventry

122

Sparks

As the moon beamed down on the silent, peaceful Earth, with great care, he lifted up the fragile wooden stick which blazed with flying colours and, as cautiously as a ballerina's touch, he patted the star-filled tip. Everyone flamed with amazement … the sparkler was alight!

Demi Yip (11)
Norfolk House School, Birmingham

Aliens!

They came closer and closer towards me and one soon grabbed me from behind. Their faces made a shiver tingle down my spine.
I wanted to escape, I really did. I tried so hard to run but my legs wouldn't move. They were aliens … Thank goodness, it was a dream!

Symrun Samria (11)
Norfolk House School, Birmingham

124

The Knockout

It was the boxing championship. It was me and a man I never knew. I whacked him hard on the face. Luckily he hadn't fallen down. I had the same health as him. The guy threw his fists and I was down!
I got angry and turned the PS2 off!

Anish Sudera (11)
Norfolk House School, Birmingham

125

It's Magic

'Get him!' the bullies shouted.
I fell to the ground as the bullies hit me. Then I
felt the magic burst through me!
I flew up to the heavens with my angel wings,
they can't catch me now, I thought.
I shot them with my laser eyes saying, 'Take
that!'

Kyna Dixon (11)
Norfolk House School, Birmingham

The Little Pony

'Come on Mum!' Hannah shouted.
Hannah's mum ran downstairs ready.
When they got to the stable Hannah picked out
a shabby grey pony. They took the pony home
with them and on the way they saw a magic
pony book.
Later Hannah whispered magic words …
Her pony was a unicorn!

Simran Sirpal (10)
Norfolk House School, Birmingham

The Raging Seaman

Fear gripped my heart as I voyaged through the Atlantic Ocean. Like a stag being pursued by the hounds of Hell into the midwinter wastes of the ocean. Clouds encircled me as the omen sailed by.
Suddenly a colossal chain ripped the sky apart. Manoeuvring into a cold abyss, diminishing!

Saad Lakhani (11)
Norfolk House School, Birmingham

128

Monster Eggs

Buzz! The machine shot into action, making eggs, monster eggs. I watched, awe-struck, as the creatures emerged covered in fluorescent goo!

One by one they marched towards me. I was surrounded! I backed against a wall, spotting a button.

Bang! I pressed the button, the machine exploded, slaughtering the monsters!

Alex Parry (10)
Priors Field Primary School, Kenilworth

129

The Kitchen Monster

He approached the kitchen door, tiptoeing
all the way. He listened hard. He heard the
faint sound of a knife being sharpened in the
background!
He closed his eyes, stepped into the kitchen;
the sound was getting louder.
'Good day at school? I'm about to cut the meat.
Your meat!'

Andrew Kirkwood (10)
Priors Field Primary School, Kenilworth

Lost

I woke up from the black. People all around me,
a cave? Strange drifting noises everywhere,
a man with eyes aback his forehead, was I
dreaming?
Drawings on the walls, done with blood. In the
corner of my eye, a glimpse of light above.
I realised … I was dead!

Amy Gravett (10)
Priors Field Primary School, Kenilworth

I Don't Taste Good

It was in front of me. It was hungry. Its teeth like knives. I slipped through a gap in the teeth. It was pitch-black. It did not like the taste. I did not get to the digestive system.
It growled, 'You are late for school.'

Joseph Villiers-Dunn (10)
Priors Field Primary School, Kenilworth

132

How Hedgehogs Got Their Spikes

The hedgehogs were in a forest. Suddenly a hungry fox appeared! The smallest hedgehog hid in a prickly field. When the fox went away they all came out. The small hedgehog had spikes!
'Where are the spikes from?'
'In that field,' he said.
They all rolled in!

Emma Burrows (10)
Priors Field Primary School, Kenilworth

Turbo Teacher

I was walking into class when I noticed Class 4 being taught about the turbo engine. It was irresistible not to press the 'on' switch! I sneakily walked up behind the teacher and pressed the button! The teacher noisily crashed through the roof and the kids shouted, 'No more lessons!'

William Vickery (10)
Priors Field Primary School, Kenilworth

A Spell That Goes Wrong

Rebecca liked making magic spells. She was an inventive girl. One day she made a spell and tried some new ingredients. She put in flower petals, snakes and pencils. It looked good and she couldn't wait to see what it turned out like. It exploded onto the floor!

Abbie Bennett (10)
Priors Field Primary School, Kenilworth

135

Scaredy Cat

I was walking my dog in the park. I didn't want
to go because I was scared of the monster! The
deadly monster's teeth were bared when I met
him by the lake!
As I sprinted home I wondered why I was so
scared of cats!

Timothy Griew (10)
Priors Field Primary School, Kenilworth

The Yeti

The party in the Himalayas was starting. *Ding-dong* went the doorbell. Tom peeped round the door. A yeti growled at him! He screamed. The abominable snowman's head fell to the floor revealing a young boy!
'Happy birthday, Tom!' shouted Matt, Tom's friend!

Sabrina Evans (10)
Priors Field Primary School, Kenilworth

137

Alien Landing

Zzoomm! A spaceship came flying down and landed. Out stepped the alien. 'Earthlings, face my wrath,' shouted the alien; KZ7. 'I will destroy your race. Ha, ha, ha, ha, ha!' KZ7 laughed evilly.

Suddenly, *splat!*

The alien said, 'Oh dung beetle.' It died.

'Die mosquito!' said an evil voice.

Samuel McKinnon (10)
Priors Field Primary School, Kenilworth

A Magical Spell That Goes Wrong, Or Doesn't

The potion was swirling and circling round, coloured green, purple, even amber. 'Hold on,' said Mary, 'the spell looks wrong. Bubble and boil, oh magic stew, make my special wish come true.'
This time it worked but Mary's wish was secret. Soon after she revealed her secret, 'I'm a witch!'

Emma Bolshaw (10)
Priors Field Primary School, Kenilworth

A Spell Goes Wrong

I have to do it. I have to read the spell.
Now everything is falling apart, but what's this
word?
'Stop!'
Everything stops.
'I am not going to read that again, let's get out
of here!'

Matthew Bunting (10)
Priors Field Primary School, Kenilworth

140

Dinner Time

I was surrounded by killer sharks. I got out my laser gun and started shooting! Finally the boss shark appeared. I got out my super pearl-firing bazooka and …
'Tommy, dinner's ready!'
'Oh Mum, just five more minutes.'
'OK, just five more minutes.'
'Thanks Mum!' So anyway and … *Game over!*

Robert Joesbury (10)
Priors Field Primary School, Kenilworth

141

The Scary Cheese

I was walking down the street. Suddenly I heard something following me! A cheese beast jumped out! I ran fast but the cheese beast ran faster. It got really close and ate me!
I woke up in my bed and thought, *I wish I hadn't eaten that cheese last night!*

Matthew Slater (10)
Priors Field Primary School, Kenilworth

A Magic Spell

Mix it up, stir it round. Make a spell that conjures … Achoo! Miaow! my cat said.
I went and made a cup of tea and grabbed a biscuit. It was strange, I couldn't see my hand. Then I realised I had made a spell that made me invisible.
'Oops! Help!'

Amy Williams (10)
Priors Field Primary School, Kenilworth

143

The Snowman Ran Away

It was a snowy day, we went out to play. We decided to make a snowman, then we went inside for a cup of cocoa and then went back out to play.
We looked here, there and everywhere but the snowman was nowhere to be found!

Anna Thomas (9)
Priors Field Primary School, Kenilworth

The Haunted Castle

My heart was pounding. My eyes pierced open. The castle … was haunted! The trees were whistling in my ears whilst the wind was screaming!
Suddenly, the window shattered; I ran, not looking back. A beam of light in front of me, I charged on forwards and out of the door!

Serena Bird (10)
Priors Field Primary School, Kenilworth

The Black Dog

On the cold street Tom stood. He didn't know
where he was. Something moved, 'Hello,
anyone there?' Tom said. Then he realised why
nobody was on the street. There stood a great
black dog, its teeth bared!
'You there, come in quickly!'
Tom quickly hurried through the door,
very relieved.

James Scott (10)
Priors Field Primary School, Kenilworth

Speeding Teacher

I'm Hannah and I'm going to tell you the story
of the day Anna died.
It was a sweltering day and we were going for a
run, when suddenly Anna ran out into the road.
Then I heard it. Her deafening scream!
She had been hit by our speeding teacher!

Hannah Jones (10)
Priors Field Primary School, Kenilworth

My Crazy Experiment

I'm a scientist working in my lab. What I'm going to do today, is something very mad. If it goes wrong it will blow the roof off my wonderful lab.
But I am very happy that I am not that bad!

Rohin Court (9)
Priors Field Primary School, Kenilworth

The Hospital

'It's very serious,' the doctor explained. 'I'll have to put you on special treatment. It sometimes has side effects.' He handed me a prescription, 'Take this to your local supermarket.'
'Why not the chemist?' I asked.
'Read it. Chips and ice cream daily with terrible side effects of being fat!'

Sophia Warren (10)
Priors Field Primary School, Kenilworth

The Woods

Jack was strolling in the woods. Suddenly an owl appeared. He stopped, he looked everywhere. He ran further into the woods, then a black creature appeared. It jumped on Jack and took him to the ground. He was wounded. The wolf disappeared into darkness. Jack was never seen again.

William Yarwood (10)
Robin Hood Primary School, Birmingham

The Train

It went fast, then it was extremely slow, it was about to stop. Then something started to howl. As it was howling something was moving and touching my back. It was very dark.
I opened my eyes, it was in the big park.

Aroosa Mirza (9)
Robin Hood Primary School, Birmingham

151

In The Woods

There he lay in the dead of night, all he heard was the howling wind. Then he heard a crack in a bush, he checked it out.

'Argh.'

A minute later he found himself running for his life.

Suddenly, 'Boo,' Harry stumbled to his feet.

'Harry, time for school darling.'

Dayle Powell (10)
Robin Hood Primary School, Birmingham

152

The Mystery Ghost

There he lay awake on his couch licking the
blood and said, 'Boo, ba, loo, la.'
Then I heard a bang and a thump. I was filled
with fear.
He saw and invited me.
I was terrified, sweat trickled down my spine but
it was all a dream.

Hamzaa Amjad (9)
Robin Hood Primary School, Birmingham

153

The Killer Slide

I climbed the stairs. It was all fine then I saw
it. It was where she died. I sat on the slide of
kill. I could see my parents waving below me. I
couldn't, but a great force pushed me. I fell …
'Wake up Hatim,' said my mum.

Hatim Hassanali (10)
Robin Hood Primary School, Birmingham

Dolphin Troubles

There lived a dolphin called Sam. One day she was gliding majestically through the gleaming water when she saw a diver in the water. The shadow lurked. What was it ...? A diver came up to the surface with a big bucketful of fresh fish.

Charlotte Winder (9)
Robin Hood Primary School, Birmingham

Hallowe'en

It was a dark Hallowe'en night.
I was sick and tired of people knocking on our house door and children asking for sweets. I had had enough.
Suddenly a loud knock came and it was a headless ghost!
'Grrrr, ahhhh.'
Phew, it was just my friend Tim, 'Scary.'

Jay Vadukul (10)
Robin Hood Primary School, Birmingham

The Daydreamer

Me and my cousin went to Alton Towers. It's everything I've ever dreamed of.
After a fantastic ride, I stopped in my tracks. I could see a shape. Nervously I dared to look. Then I saw it, my favourite ride ever, 'The Swingers'.

Daniella McDonald (10)
Robin Hood Primary School, Birmingham

157

Funfair

Dad and I strolled around the park. I stopped
dead. Where was Dad? Sweat started pouring
down my face. I turned around, he was
nowhere to be seen. What was that? It gave me
the shivers. I was getting really scared.
'Come on Jordan, do you want some
candyfloss?'

Alex Phelan (10)
Robin Hood Primary School, Birmingham

The Attack

I got home and knocked the door, no answer
so I got the key from the secret place and
unlocked it.
I saw Mum lying on the floor. I rushed over
to her. I heard footsteps upstairs. I got up,
someone opened the door and grabbed me.
'Argh!'

Natasha Taheem (10)
Robin Hood Primary School, Birmingham

The Incompetent Witch

The witch, Wobbly, was making a spell. She was doing a spell about hair and it all went wrong. Her hair fell out and her cat's.
She reversed the spell but nothing happened. She put the strongest potion that she had, and then it went back to normal.

Shannon Stevens (10)
Robin Hood Primary School, Birmingham

At World's End

Suddenly an ear-splitting crash shattered silence. Tears rolled down my cheeks. People wept, running from the terror. I frantically looked for my family. They were cuddled together and I joined. I saw people looking for their family.

'Iqra, wake up.'

It was Mum. It was a dream. Thank God.

Iqra Khan (10)
Robin Hood Primary School, Birmingham

161

A Magic Spell That Goes Wrong

One day there was an evil witch that wanted to cast a spell that would put an end to the world. This spell took hundreds of years to make.
It exploded.
'Argh!' I woke up. 'Witch go away, don't put an end to the world.'
Oh it was just a dream.

Lemar Chandegra (10)
Robin Hood Primary School, Birmingham

162

Falling Star

Once I had a dream, that I was a falling star
coming back from Heaven.
It was six months since my brother had died.
It felt weird.
I was falling from the sky, I was shouting, 'Help.'
Sometimes when I closed my eyes, I could still
be with him forever.

Josie Brookes (11)
Rounds Green Primary School, Oldbury

163

Marshmallow Bobby

He walked anxiously forward seven steps to gather his weekly food. *Bang, bang, bang!* his giant chubby marshmallow feet echoed throughout the town.

'Daniel,' shouted Kelly, 'why are you banging your feet in our new kitchen?'

'Mommy, why didn't you feed me? I'm really hungry.'

'Oh I'm really sorry Bob.'

Kelsey Ashmore (11)
Rounds Green Primary School, Oldbury

My Nightmare

I was frightened. I was home alone, the door creaked open. Suddenly I heard footsteps coming closer to me. I took a deep breath … I got closer to the copper-brown door. I stopped … I took a big step back … Then I closed my eyes tightly … 'Mum!'

Audrey Dhlamini (10)
Rounds Green Primary School, Oldbury

Time

Everywhere I go I hear *tick-tock, tick-tock.* The clock, it won't stop. Day and night *tick-tock, tick-tock.* I walk out the house, it is still in my head. The clock strikes ten, it is getting closer. 'Come on Jordan, it's bedtime,' shouted Mom calmly.

Luke Downing (10)
Rounds Green Primary School, Oldbury

The Haunted Mansion

I knocked on the door, *creak*. It opened and an old man appeared out of the mist. He pointed to the door. I walked to it, the old man pushed me into the room and locked the door. I was trapped with nowhere to go.
'Damn! Game over.'

Raj Sangha (11)
Rounds Green Primary School, Oldbury

Untitled

It's the FA Cup Final between Arsenal and
Manchester United. Thierry Henry has been
awarded with a fantastic free-kick right at the
edge of the area. Is he gonna score or not? Are
they gonna be the winners of the FA Cup Final?
Find out, after the break.

Anderson Ongono (11)
Rounds Green Primary School, Oldbury

Bingo Grandma

My gran is a whizz at Bingo.
Every single night she's always going home
with a jar of money in her prize-winning hands
looking so brave and mighty. Suddenly Gran
said, 'Uncle Bob stop stealing my pocket
money you Bingo thief. I couldn't even trust you
with money.'

Jordan Burrell (10)
Rounds Green Primary School, Oldbury

The Book That Came To Life

It was quiet. The only noise was the *pitter-patter* of the raindrops hitting the roof of the tent. Suddenly, there was a deep inhuman growling. I carefully crept to the door of the tent. I screamed. My parents came rushing in. It was lucky … it was only a book.

Jennifer Green (9)
St Benedict's Catholic Primary School, Atherstone

The Spell That Went Wrong!

Hi, I'm Jenna and I'm a witch. I'm doing some witch work at the minute. Spells and potions are the best, usually it goes wrong for me but today it hasn't. *Bang!* I think I spoke too soon.

Jenna Allison (9)
St Benedict's Catholic Primary School, Atherstone

The Spooky Story

I was trembling so much my knees clashed together. As the monster crept through the door I felt a cold chill down my spine. A loud scream slipped out of my mouth. My parents came in, but I was OK. The book I was reading scared me. It was scary.

Jake Hargreaves (9)
St Benedict's Catholic Primary School, Atherstone

Horrific

I was standing sheepishly. There were strange figures standing all around. Houses looked spooky and ancient. There were cobwebs and monster people. Everyone was out of their houses. It was getting dark. Nervously I stood until a hand touched me, and wished me 'Happy Hallowe'en.' Wow!

Gabriela Morton (9)
St Benedict's Catholic Primary School, Atherstone

173

The Man That Stood On The Empire State Building

An extremely short time ago there was a man. He was on the Empire State Building. He fell out of the window and had to have his arm amputated. All blood spurted out. The medics came in an ambulance. Too late he was gone!

Toby Stevens (8)
St Benedict's Catholic Primary School, Atherstone

174

Zombie Island

I am on Zombie Island with Scooby-Doo and the gang. We are investigating why lots of people are disappearing. We already know from Velma's laptop that zombies live here. Pirates used to sail these waters and their spirits stayed here. We are going into the woods to investigate.

Alexander Currie (9)
St Benedict's Catholic Primary School, Atherstone

175

Cameron And His Imaginary Cars

Hi, I'm Cameron, I've won the cool million. I've got all the BMWs you can get. I've been to Bulgaria, given money to charity and lots to my family and friends.
Well, that's how it's going to be when I'm older. I'm only nine now!

Cameron Brotherhood (9)
St Benedict's Catholic Primary School, Atherstone

176

Blond Boy

There was a boy who was very young and entered a house. He saw a plate of porridge and ate it. Then he sat on a chair, then had a nap on a bed. The door opened as the family came in.

Inderpal Singh Atkar (9)
St Hubert's Catholic Primary School, Oldbury

177

Medusa Mum

I crept silently to the door with a shield and with
a mirror.
'Whaaa!' screamed someone.
I said to myself, 'I want my mummy.'
Inside, *sssss.*
'What was that? Is it a snake?'
OK. One step. I turned.
'Argh!'
'Wake up.'
'Eh?'
'Wake up, you're late for school.'
'What? Mom!'

Richard Smith (9)
St Hubert's Catholic Primary School, Oldbury

178

The Strange Sleeper Was Found ...

Early Monday morning Tom heard a noise, it was coming from downstairs.
He rushed out of bed and slowly walked downstairs. He reached the last step and found someone fast asleep in the corridor. He moved slowly to the person, he moved closer. Then, what a shock. It's James ...

Kaiytlan O'Connell (9)
St Hubert's Catholic Primary School, Oldbury

179

Lizzie Zip Mouth

I can't believe it's today. I've decided I'm
not going to talk. Not to Mum, Rory, Zack,
especially not Sam.
We had to meet this strange old lady (who's
Sam's great-gran!). I can't believe I'm saying
this, but I like her. She doesn't talk either.
Great Granny Zip Mouth!

Sanari Abeyagunaratne (9)
St Hubert's Catholic Primary School, Oldbury

Lucy Like Lighting

It was all when Lucy Like Lighting, fell in a pond. She was able to fly. She woke up and up, up, up away she flew.
The doctor came round and checked Lucy, but she was fine. Then the doctor went and aarrgghh … She fell in the pond again.

Olivia Stevens (9)
St Hubert's Catholic Primary School, Oldbury

181

The Wrong Spell

Well here I am, a boring person, *buff!* I can't believe my eyes. I wish I was a pop star, *buff!* I don't feel like a pop star. I'm an ugly frog! I can't show myself off ever again.
Suddenly there was a noise, the genie was now gone. *Buff!*

Chloe Boden (9)
St Hubert's Catholic Primary School, Oldbury

Goldilocks And The Three Bears

One day a little girl went into a house and ate some porridge. Baby Bear's was lovely then she broke his chair and slept on his bed. The bears came home, she was terrified of them so she ran away and she never went to that house ever again.

Lidia Krasinkewicz (9)
St Hubert's Catholic Primary School, Oldbury

Harry Potter

The boy, Harry, with a lightning scar, went to magic school. His head held high, with an owl by his side. Harry made friends and enemies. He was in a chess game; he was courageous with friends nearby. He went through some rooms …

He finally found his enemy … his mum.

Connor Cobb (9)
St Hubert's Catholic Primary School, Oldbury

The Beast

I was relaxed then I heard something coming up the stairs. *What was that?* I thought. The door opened.
'Ra!'
'Argh, it's a beast, stay back,' I said.
'Ha, ha, ha,' the beast was laughing then I realised it was just my little brother.

Ashpal Virdee (9)
St Hubert's Catholic Primary School, Oldbury

185

One Spooky Night

It was dark when I awoke with a start. A loud yelling filled my ears and a gloomy shadow stood at the window. I was scared, I crept slowly towards the window, closer, nearer and nearer still. Suddenly I ripped the curtain open, it was Tuffy, my cat.

Charlotte Smith (8)
St James' Junior School, Bulkington

186

One Spooky Night

It was dark when I awoke with a start. There was a screeching in my bedroom. It was getting louder and closer as I pulled the cover over my head.
I got out of bed and crept to the window. I pulled open the curtain, there was my cat scratching.

Sam Gisbourne (8)
St James' Junior School, Bulkington

187

One Spooky Night

It was dark when I awoke with a start. I thought I was dreaming but there I heard it again. It got louder, louder and closer. It sounded like a wolf howling at the moonlight. Then I heard a scratching at my door.
I opened my door. 'Ahh it's Meg!'

Annabel Cadman (8)
St James' Junior School, Bulkington

One Spooky Night

It was dark when I awoke with a start. I saw a giant thing, it got closer. I pulled the cover over my head, it screeched. I jumped out of bed. It cornered me next to the window. I looked in, it was a branch casting a shadow.

Tom Jones (8)
St James' Junior School, Bulkington

The Bad Night

It was dark, what was it? What was that noise?
There it was again, *tap, tap, tap.* I tried to cover
my ears, it didn't work.
Suddenly a shadow appeared, it got closer. In
the blink of an eye, it dashed under my bed but
it was just my cat.

Matthew Cooke (8)
St James' Junior School, Bulkington

One Spooky Night

It was dark when I awoke with a start.
Something was creaking up the stairs and it got
closer, even more close to my door. I pulled my
covers over head, started to shake. I lifted my
head up slowly, a giant shadow crept over. It
was my brother, laughing.

Marsha Cowley (8)
St James' Junior School, Bulkington,

191

One Spooky Night

It was dark when I awoke with a start.
Something was tapping at my window. I pulled
the cover over my head. I took a deep breath
and got up slowly. 'What was it?'
I got closer.
The noise got louder, I stripped the curtains
open and saw my cat.

Estelle Richards (8)
St James' Junior School, Bulkington

192

One Spooky Night

It was dark when I awoke with a start. I heard
something. There it was again but louder.
What was it?
I saw a shadow. I hid under the covers. Then
I crept out of bed to the window and opened
the curtains. There was Angel, my pet cat,
scratching.

Abby Masters (7)
St James' Junior School, Bulkington

193

One Spooky Night

It was a dark night. I awoke with a start. I heard whining downstairs. Then it stepped on the first step on the stairs.

Suddenly a shadow appeared, it looked like a ten foot wolf. It gratefully sneaker closer. then it turned around the corner, it was my dog.

George Patrick
St James' Junior School, Bulkington

194

Doctor Who Vs The Robot Servants

King Henry's robot servants were back and they were ready to invade the world! King Henry wasn't pleased, the TARDIS had just landed in his field outside his palace, a gunshot was fired from the top window, it hit Martha.

'No,' shouted the Doctor! 'I'll come back for you, promise!'

Sophie Edwards (11)
St Peter's CE Primary School, Birmingham

195

Three Little Donkeys

There once were three donkeys. The first donkey built his house from straw and a wolf blew it down. That donkey ran to the other donkey's house. The wolf blew that house down too. Those donkeys ran to the house made from bricks and the wolf couldn't blow it down.

James Cross (11)
St Peter's CE Primary School, Birmingham

Live Or Die?

Bang! Grandpa got hit by the car.
When we got in the ambulance, I thought,
*we were just walking home from school when
suddenly it happened.*
As we arrived at the hospital he got rushed to
theatre.
After the operation something happened, but
what?

Chloe Kalirai (11)
St Peter's CE Primary School, Birmingham

The Giant

One day Tom was sleeping in his garden.
Suddenly, a giant appeared out of nowhere and
started to crush buildings, even Tom's house.
He could hear people crying.
Tom was under a load of rubble, he could hear
his mum shouting, 'Tom, wake up!'
It was all a dream.

Victor Bulso (11)
St Peter's CE Primary School, Birmingham

Little Red Riding Hood

The little girl walked along in her red cloak until she came to her grandma's cottage! She looked rather different with her big yellow eyes, sharp pointy teeth until it was all revealed. 'You didn't think I was a real wolf?' said the soft voice of her grandma.

Emma Stone (11)
St Peter's CE Primary School, Birmingham

199

Crash!

'No! Don't!' She ran out in front of the car.
There was a scream; I went over to see if she
was alive, or not. 'Speak to me Sasha,' I said to
her, but she didn't answer.
'Mandy, put the book down and go to sleep.'
'OK Mum.'

Megan Macgowan (11)
St Peter's CE Primary School, Birmingham

200

The Box

One day a light glowed in a house down the
street. A boy called Tom ran to the house to find
a box. He opened it and there were the most
beautiful jewels ever. What would he do?

Steven Mapp (11)
St Peter's CE Primary School, Birmingham

201

Ring Of Faith

The first thing I saw was the smoke, thick grey clouds of it … the stable was on fire. Would Star trust me enough to walk through the flames? She trusted me, I could see it in her eyes. I can picture her now … looking down from a corner of Heaven.

Bryony Loveless (10)
St Peter's CE Primary School, Birmingham

The Big Fall

Argh! Jack was falling down a very deep ditch, with razor-sharp spikes at the bottom. Then he remembered he had turbo rockets underneath his shoes, instantly he put them on and luckily he melted the spikes. Then he tried to escape, but did he?

Imandeep Sihre (11)
St Peter's CE Primary School, Birmingham

203

A Sparkle,
A Shine, A Fizz

Natasha looked out of her bedroom window. A sparkle … a shine … a fizz. She quickly ran downstairs and to the bottom of her garden. A sparkle … a shine … a fizz. Natasha's face turned pale.

'Hello, who was that?' She turned … she screamed … she ran. This was no dream.

Lydia Carrington (10)
St Peter's CE Primary School, Birmingham

204

Back From The Dead

One day last year, a man called Dave Colling
was stabbed in the heart.
When Dave's parents went to the graveyard
they heard a noise. They thought the same.
Dave groaned! They looked at each other in
shock and leaned over Dave's grave.
They knew they were being extraordinarily
ridiculous.

Chelsea Tomlinson (11)
Shirestone Community School, Birmingham

205

Flaming Miracle Of The Sky

Year 3045, World War V.
'Marine squad move out!' shouted Lt Baker.
That was 3 years ago, now I'm a Lt with Jordan.
We're on the east coast of the Sahara Desert.
'Daleks 12 o'clock, fire, fire.'
'We are your demise,' screeched Dalk.
Dalk, the most supreme, vicious steel mutant
being!

Adam Askew (10)
Shirestone Community Primary School, Birmingham

Question?

My friends played a prank on me, and that's why I'm here!
999, one of the numbers that was dialled on this dark night.
The police turned up, to find a man walking outside and took him away. He was soon to realise his fate! He had committed a crime, unfortunately.

Hollie Merrix (10)
Shirestone Community Primary School, Birmingham

Troy

Rain poured. During the rowing the Greeks encountered the beach of Troy! Arrows came from the sky! The Greeks prepared for battle, they touched the moist sands of the beach. The soldiers of Greece charged up the beach killing everyone.
The Trojans' beach was defeated, but the war wasn't over.

Sam Tranter (11)
Shirestone Community Primary School, Birmingham

Deep In The Forest

Katie struggled through the forest. Night fell. Suddenly, a branch fell on her shoulder and the tree held her still.

'Hello,' said a deep voice. The ancient oak tree was speaking.

After a thoughtful, deep conversation, Katie decided to live with the forest away from other humans, who were unpeaceful.

Amy Hooper (11)
Shirestone Community Primary School, Birmingham

Zoey 101

After a long stressful day of school Zoey, Hannah and Swifty had nothing better to do but look at the 'fit' Logan Rease.
The next morning it was Hannah's chemistry test. She got a D+, she wasn't happy with this grade so she asked Logan to tutor her, in shyness.

Hannah Elliott (11)
Shirestone Community Primary School, Birmingham

Kensuke's Kingdom

The boy fell off the boat and could feel his goose pimples rising all over.
He saw a huge shiny spoon coming down from the clouds. Then he was pulled around in circles by this spoon. He saw the water turning brown and a humongous hairy lip sipping the water.

Leila Spencer (10)
The Croft School, Stratford-upon-Avon

The Scary Picture

My legs shaking with fear. My feet keep on
thinking of running.
I hear a loud noise in my ear, sweat gathers
on my back. It feels like a nightmare except
even Mum is scared. It's worse than my dog's
tongue licking my face.
My eyes open. It's grandad!

Joshua Fox (10)
The Croft School, Stratford-upon-Avon

Portugal, Our Holiday

Day one: Arrived in Portugal. It was a hot, sunny day. We could see the sea from Faro airport. We travelled until we reached the villa.
Day two: We went swimming with friends.
Day three: We went on a banana-boat in the sea. Lost goggles.
Day four: Went home.

Pippa Beharrell (10)
The Croft School, Stratford-upon-Avon

213

The Pink Pineapple

The pink pineapple lived in a pineapple tree, but unfortunately it was the only pink one. It lived unhappily because no one would play with it. It leaped and yelled to try and get a bit of attention.
Then it turned yellow.
It was the happiest pineapple on the Earth!

Alice Vaudry (10)
The Croft School, Stratford-upon-Avon

My Disaster

'Grandad?'
'Yes, darling?'
'Where is the toilet?'
'Right over there.'
'Can you come?'
'No,' Grandad said.
As I started walking, sweat trickled down my
back. In the toilets, I went, but to my horror,
weird buckets were stuck to the wall!
Then I realised! 'Grandad!' I screamed!

Maisy Geddes (10)
The Croft School, Stratford-upon-Avon

My Disaster

We arrived in France hot and sticky and went to have a shower. By the time I had come out, it was 8pm.
We went to the swimming pool, met a new friend and played for ages. Then the disaster happened, I fell down a ditch in front of everyone!

Sarah Wheeler (10)
The Croft School, Stratford-upon-Avon

At Home

The floor creaks, the shower leaks and I am
bored. My house is boring!
'Mum! Mum! I want a dog please.'
'I will think about it.'
'Mum! I want a bunny please.'
'Wait. Let me ask Dad. Bob, he now wants a
bunny.'
'Okay, fine, let's get one.'
'Thanks Dad.'

George Sagar (10)
The Croft School, Stratford-upon-Avon

Cinders

Cinders opened the oven with shock, a cloud of mist flooded the kitchen, the fairy godmother emerged. She waved her wand!
Cinders danced at the ball until the clock chimed twelve, then appeared back in the kitchen.
The prince visited her house. The shoe fitted, they lived together for evermore!

Holly Sutton (10)
The Ridge Primary School, Stourbridge

218

What On Earth Happened?

Crash! It was silent for about ten minutes, until Penny found herself lying down in an ambulance. All she could hear was flashing sirens. Penny closed her eyes and fell into a deep sleep!
Next thing she knew, she was lying in bed at home.
What on earth happened?

Lydia Crump (10)
The Ridge Primary School, Stourbridge

Alien!

The spaceship hovered silently over Jim's
house. Inside they looked for their next victim.
Jim fitted the kill within seconds. Jim found
himself on-board the ship. Jim banged furiously
on the window shouting for help.
The alien laughed as the ship hovered on its
journey into space!

Joshua Reynolds (10)
The Ridge Primary School, Stourbridge

The Creature

'Deep underground was a creature with teeth like pins and gooey green skin, nobody made a sound. It's all silent apart from one cricket in the background and then he grabs you, and nobody will ever see you agai- …'
'Mum, where are you? Where are you Mum?'

Beth Tibbetts (10)
The Ridge Primary School, Stourbridge

221

The Easter Thief

Jane slowly opened the creaky door on that
one Easter morning.
'The Easter eggs are gone!' she shouted.
'No they haven't,' explained Dad, he'd taken the
eggs for an Easter egg hunt.
'Silly me,' laughed Jane.
'It was all I could do on this special Easter Day,'
laughed Dad.

Bethany Herrington (10)
The Ridge Primary School, Stourbridge

Alone

Michael opened his eyes. Everywhere was deserted. Creepy faces. Michael saw he was surrounded by aliens, he couldn't do anything. They took him to their base. He was transformed into an alien, they were taking over the Earth.
Nuclear bombs were planted everywhere. The Earth was destroyed.

Brodie Williams (9)
The Ridge Primary School, Stourbridge

Last Invention

Dr Short Story is inventing the Bookotron 500.
'Just insert the dictionary in its head. I shall rule
every library in town!'
He tested it out (it didn't go well!)
'That's all for today, now it's beddie time!'
But he forgot to switch it off.
Oh no Robot's fallen down!

Jessica Heatherley (11)
The Ridge Primary School, Stourbridge

The Spaceship
Has Landed

'The spaceship has landed Sir.'
'Where has it landed?'
'It's landed on the coast of Porth.'
'What does he look like?'
'He's alien with a body like a crab, he's with an army.'
'What are they armed with?'
'Sonic blasters.'
What are they?'
'They are destructive.'
Bang! Nothing is left.

Ben Nightingale (10)
The Ridge Primary School, Stourbridge

225

Alien Invasion!

Bang! 'What was that?'
'A spaceship in our garden.'
'Moommmm … Mom, come quickly.'
'What is it now?'
'It's an alien.'
'Where? There's no such thing, *argh!* It's
creeping towards us!'
The alien pointed his crooked finger towards
them, a bright light suddenly beamed at them.
They vanished into thin air …

Ellie Humphries (10)
The Ridge Primary School, Stourbridge

The Muffin Man

An evil baker planned to bake a gingerbread man. He baked the biggest gingerbread man in the world.
The gingerbread man came to life. *Crash! Bang! Boom!* The gingerbread man started wrecking the city, people were devastated. The gingerbread man wrecked, destroyed and demolished the city.

Mark Tandy (10)
The Ridge Primary School, Stourbridge

It's Alive!

'It moved Sir!'
'Excellent!' The robot sat.
The professor bellowed, 'It's alive. I'll call it
Killer Robo 7000!'
The robot stood and walked towards the
assistant.
RIP! The robot sliced the assistant in half!
He walked towards the professor, then the
robot stopped and fell. *Bang!*
'Phew!' the professor said.

Kyle Gardiner (10)
The Ridge Primary School, Stourbridge

228

Aliens Attack

Boom! Crash! Aliens attack.
'Aliens! They're here.'
Bang!
'What is that creature?'
'I don't know but we need to get out of here.'
No! Lightning.'
'We are all going to die.'
Bombs dropping, people dying.
The country is being overruled by aliens!
Everybody died and no one survived.

Alex Bodin (9)
The Ridge Primary School, Stourbridge

The Disaster Spell

'I'm bored,' groaned Molly.
'I've got an idea,' Grace burst out. 'I was thinking we could make a potion, to go where you like,' Grace explained.
'Finished,' said Grace.
'Let's try it,' said Molly. 'Here we go!' Molly shouted.
'Wow.'
'How do we get back?'
'Don't know.'
'Argh!' they screamed.

Aprille Smith (10)
The Ridge Primary School, Stourbridge

At The Vet's

I'm going to the vet's with my dog Polly. She
has a problem with her leg.
Her vet, Molly, she helps all the time. Polly
has to have an operation, she has to have a
bandage because she can't touch it.
We go to see Polly the next day.

Amy Fincher (10)
The Ridge Primary School, Stourbridge

231

Happy Holiday?

The engines started with a roar and soon we were hurtling down the runway.
After a few peaceful moments, flying over trees and rivers, the engines froze. Screams rang out, as the plane fell like a dead bird.
The engines spluttered and the plane continued its silent journey.

Sarah Alebon (9)
The Ridge Primary School, Stourbridge

232

Thump!

Thump! I pulled the bedcovers up to my nose.
It was coming closer.
Thump! I screamed, flung open the door,
jumped from my bed and saw my incredibly
ferocious pet kittens having a great time
tumbling down the stairs.
Oh well. At least they're not going to eat my
brains!

Rosie Hierons (10)
The Ridge Primary School, Stourbridge

Night-Time

The door opened slowly. It was pitch-black.
I couldn't see a thing. Voices echoed from
outside. I sat up in bed, breathing slowly. Soft
steps getting closer.
Then, 'Argh!' Sharp claws grabbed onto my
pyjama top followed by a scratching on my
face.
Miaow! That blooming cat.

Robert Johnston (10)
The Ridge Primary School, Stourbridge

234

The Death Of Humpty Dumpty

Oh what a mess, all of Humpty's egg shell all over the floor.
Rushing to the hospital. 'Please tell us he's going to live!'
They wait for the doctor to hear the bad news.
At his funeral all his bits and pieces are shown as they bury Humpty Dumpty.

Gemma Moore (10)
The Ridge Primary School, Stourbridge

235

Information

We hope you have enjoyed reading this book - and that you will continue to enjoy it in the coming years.

If you like reading and writing, drop us a line or give us a call and we'll send you a free information pack. Alternatively visit our website at www.youngwriters.co.uk

Write to:
Young Writers Information,
Remus House,
Coltsfoot Drive,
Peterborough,
PE2 9JX
Tel: (01733) 890066
Email: youngwriters@forwardpress.co.uk